Love, Live, Forgive

The Beauty of Life Arcs Toward Forgiveness

Alice-Marie Allen

Fulton Books
Meadville, PA

Published by Fulton Books 2023

ISBN 979-8-88731-499-0 (paperback)
ISBN 979-8-88731-500-3 (digital)

Printed in the United States of America

*Stricken is the beauty hidden
Behind the cast of light.
Torn to breach the breath
Of a new morning.
Unaware of the guidelines of life
That are imposed upon.
Free from the supposition of
Who one is supposed to be
The innocence of life that has
Somehow become a commodity.
What is your price to lay down,
Your life in the arms of the weary?*

*Forgiveness—forging a path to free your soul
From the battlefields of life to the
Hungers of the heart.*

Tired is the day that the boy walks the path of unknown fears. Deep inside, he feels as though he should name them and call them by what they are in the midst of his mind. Remembering back to that time, his mind trails along to another place. Broken hearts and broken spirits for the world are at war, and a Black man had to work endless days to get a glass of water.

Untrusting eyes warrant a mask of confusion. Under smoke lies a man torn and tired. Only meant to be sewn back together with the threads of a new day. This is a chapter of renewal, for the growth of a man is measured not by where he is but by where he has been. And it wasn't Disney World.

CHAPTER 1

"Grandpa, tell me a story."

"I will tell you the truths of my life that are unlike any story you've heard."

"Is it funny? Will I laugh? I want to laugh."

"I'm not saying you will split your pants, but I've got a laugh or two. If you have the time, I've got a line."

"I'm ready to listen, so go ahead," she said with anticipation.

"I see, girl, you're callin' the shots now." He smiled awkwardly and tugged at his worn green shirt. "Well, I guess I can humor you."

"Thinking back to a time when the only thought that crossed the mind of those in power was war. Now the very people we spit on and who spit on us are our very best friends. Yet, we must be careful sometimes, because the skin heals over, but the inner flesh burns with pain. Peace is a state of mind and a state of currency.

"We all fall sometimes, but it is how we get up that builds the character of a man, lady, or country."

Anesthetized by the spirits of the water, I couldn't move and could barely breathe. All I could do is hear the noises blaring in the background and see a glimmer of light shining in the distance. I told myself, "This is my destiny. This is my death." Should I come out of this alive? I shall be paralyzed with fear of living. All I knew was the war outside was nowhere as big as the battle I faced within my own body. My mind had fallen to the waste side, locked in a prison—hopeless, destitute thoughts of life unknown. But my body twitched and shook with pain, and I asked myself, "Have I been shot? And if so, where and for how long?"

"The salty bittersweet taste of blood trickled down my forehead into the barren lips of forsaken love. Then I felt it. It was my right leg, a piercing blow that can only be identified as lifelessness. Who can save me now?

Lord knows I can't save myself. Then murmurs came in a distance that grew louder and louder. Friends or foes, I thought to myself. At this point, not much mattered. They were either here to save me or finish the job. Either way, I'll be in a better state of mind than the purgatory of being a fly's dessert. Lifting up, in the air on a bed, a board, an instrument of some sort, a reassuring voice said, "You're going to be okay." Somehow, I couldn't put the pieces together of what that meant.

"Forgiveness is like learning to love yourself all over again. Knowing that the very worst part of you is good again."

THANKFULNESS

"All right, Shirley, here I go,

"When the lights of tomorrow shine at your door today, the only thought that comes to mind is thankfulness mixed with a bit of blessing. The lights flash, and all you can see are the images and memories of past rights and wrongs. Although, it's a funny thing, we often embellish the worst times of our lives in a way that allows us to remember them fondly. So I think back about the people and times in my life that I am so dearly grateful for. The times that my mom would make rice porridge on Sunday evenings, we'd eat it while watching reruns of our favorite old shows, or the loving embrace of my annoying brother and sisters when they just came home from school. Or how about that time I played hide-and-seek with my best buddies, and they never found me. Lost again—in the love of the moment—forever forgotten. These are the times and the memories that run through your mind when the light shines too early, and you don't have sunglasses."

"Grandpa, what happened after the helicopter picked you up?" Shirley erupted with anticipation.

"Hush up, girl," Grandpa Isaac stuttered with dismay.

"Lifted into the air in a helicopter, the blades swinging high above my head making that *whop whop whop* chopper sound, and all I could feel was the buzzing of uncertainty. There was no tomorrow. There was no yesterday. There were only the split seconds that could be seen when my eyes winced open. Then, I could feel myself vomit everything there ever was in my life laid out in front of me on my once-pressed uniform. These were the men that we lay down in sin to raise the tide for a better tomorrow.

"However, as a man on the ground, I was just told to fight, but they never really told us why. The chopper kept lifting, and I kept spewing the stories of my life. Who was listening was of no concern, because I was only talking out of one side of my mouth. Slurred, slumbered that was the way it's done. That was how those purple hearts are won. Beauty is the day that I wake up tomorrow and need not remember the tragedies of this day. The irony is, we were rewarded for remembering, recalling, sharing, painting, and dancing our stories that we'll do anything to forget. But I guess that was what this story is all about—learning to remember without getting lost in the past.

"See, girl, I remembered for you. Now go grab Grandpa a Coke, and I'll listen to your story. Nothing can be worse than seventh grade," Grandpa Isaac said as he wrinkled his nose.

"Okay, Grandpa, but you owe me a checker game," Shirley blurted out in a huff and a puff.

"Grab me two Cokes, and we'll play Rummy," Grandpa negotiated.

"Okay, okay," she said as she scurried off and ran back with the Cokes.

"Are you black or red?" Grandpa Isaac snickered.

"I thought you said we were playing Rummy?" Shirley said in an exasperated tone, while she patted down her curled-up matted blackish-brown hair and itched a freckle.

"I figured we'll play checkers, so you won't hustle me out of my money," Grandpa Isaac said coyly as his shriveled up deep brown hand grazed her pinkish brown arm in play. "So what's going down at that super smart school of yours?"

"Oh, nothing, just work, work, and more work. The best part of the day is using the iPads," she sang out as she advanced her red checker one spot.

"Oh, I see, those funny little computer things," Grandpa Isaac said as he maneuvered his black checker all over the board and took out two of her reds.

"Yeah, Grandpa, you have one. Mom bought it for you last Christmas," she said as she shrank in her chair pondering her next move.

"Oh, right. That iPad. Yeah, it works great. I use it for taking pictures of stuff," Grandpa Isaac said proudly as he gulped down a massive sip of his Coke. He decided to take it easy on her since he was sweeping the board.

"What stuff?" she inquired as she examined the board to make her next great move, taking one of his multitudes of black pieces on the board.

"Oh, girl, don't be ornery. You were supposed to be telling me a story," Grandpa Isaac brought her back to task.

She began to ease into her story. "Okay, yesterday in language arts, the boy I kind of like threw up all over his desk. I gave him paper towels. He was so embarrassed, but he said, 'Thank you.'"

"Sounds like the boy was sick, maybe *lovesick*."

"Grandpa, you're too funny. Mrs. Wilder said he had the flu. That's probably why he was out today. My friend Missy was going to give him a note from me, but he wasn't at school. So I think I might back out of it."

Grandpa Isaac stretched his arms and said, "Why? You feeling shy?"

Shirley tickled her ear and then cleared the board. "Yeah, I don't know. What if he doesn't like me?"

"Girl, I gotta tell you about me and your Grandma," he said with a smile as the memories brought tears to his eyes.

"Oh, I love hearing stories about her."

CHAPTER 2

"She was beautiful, dark ebony chocolate dabbed with a kiss of cocoa powder. He was in love, and he knew it. It was just after his basketball defeat by the Warriors that he decided to go get a drink at the water fountain when this beautiful girl stepped up next to him and asked if he was drinking the Nile or if she could get a sip. He grinned and said that a young lady so pure should only be drinking the finest of waters, not from a dirty old river, such as the Nile.

"She complimented him on his game. He was flattered that she had watched and noticed him. She offered him a ride home, and he told her that his dad was picking him up and he best mind his manners and be outside the gym at nine o'clock sharp. Lily, the girl he was now chatting up, asked what his dad would say if the game went into overtime. Isaac replied that there's no such thing as overtime in his father's eyes. She grinned in a pleasant manner and said that he could have her number if he wanted, and he did. This encounter was the beginning of a half-century love affair encompassing wars, marriage, kids, grand kids, and an ugly battle lost to cancer. Love would know no bounds and could only be multiplied as their family grew."

"Grandma always told me you begged her to go out with you," Shirley confronted him.

Grandpa Isaac sighed with a dazed look upon his face and replied, "She'd like to think so."

"So Grandma asked you out?"

"That's how it went down, sugar," he said as he stroked his chin. "Your Grandma Lily was a bold character. She never took nothing from nobody."

The years melded into one, Grandpa Isaac remembered back to the days of their lovers' youth, but thoughts of last year's vicious battle would creep in with the haunting effects of seeing her once curvy vivacious body whittled down to nothing. Oh, how he loved to stroke her backside with a coy little tap of love and playfulness. Now he found solitude in the companionship of his granddaughter.

"Grandpa, do you think Grandma is in heaven dancing with the clouds?"

"I sure as hell hope so!"

"What are you two getting on about?" Sequoia, Shirley's mom and Grandpa Isaac's eldest daughter, asked as she sneakily skirted into the room.

"Nothing, Mom. We were just talking about Grandma." However, Shirley regretted her truthfulness when she saw her mom's big gulp and water brimming at the corners of her eyes.

"I was just telling some stories, you know how we do. Is dinner on?" Grandpa Isaac always knew how to change the subject in the nick of time before doomsday or Hades all clattered into one.

"Of course, I wouldn't want to send you two to bed hungry, we're having chicken and rice, and Alex will be home soon."

"That milkshake of a man."

"Now, Dad, don't you get started."

"I love my beautiful Oreo of a granddaughter, but that white bread, good for nothing." Grandpa Isaac's remarks may seem off the cuff and even a bit racist, but there is context for everything. Grandpa Isaac can't help but remember last year when they were in the midst of their tragedy. That foolish man, Alex, decided to step out on his fifteen-year marital commitment.

Sequoia was always the apple of her father's eye, being the first and only daughter. He could remember the first moments when her little hand curled around his finger, and from that moment on, he was taken. He had always had reservations about Alex and his daughter's union, but since the loss of Grandma Lily and Grandpa's move into their big lofty house, times have been tense. Alex was always a handsome matter-of-fact man who had provided above and beyond for his family but yearned for comfort when comfort wasn't there.

Sequoia held on, and Alex showered her with sorrys and flowers, but somehow the wounds remained fresh. Grandpa Isaac somehow could forgive Vietnam, forgive his country, but couldn't tolerate or utter a word of forgiveness to his son by marriage. Shirley remained oblivious to the turmoil and thought Grandpa was just being the jokester that he always was, nothing new.

"Dinner's ready!" Sequoia rang out. "Please wash up well before sitting down at the table. Okay, Shirley, we don't want to spread those schoolyard germs."

"All right, Mama, but please don't nag, I'm starting to get a headache from being irritated by you," Shirley announced.

Grandpa Isaac stepped outside to have a little puff of his pipe. He chose not to smoke cigarettes, but occasionally, he liked to indulge in his pipe. Alex pulled in the driveway at six o'clock on the dot, in his pimped-out silver sedan that was really nothing but a family car with charcoal gray interior. He climbed out of the car with a long-lean swagger with his chiseled features and sandy skin complementing his tousled auburn hair that curled under just a little too long for Grandpa Isaac's liking.

"How goes it?" Alex asked in a casual West Coast kind of way. Grandpa Isaac was born and raised in Virginia, a southern East Coast state with hospitality in a formalized way. The two men, sometimes boys, couldn't have been more different than night and day. The bridge between them consisted of two females, one a girl and one a lady of the house. Sequoia and Shirley knew how to play nice and were always offering peace treaties.

Interestingly enough, Sequoia and Alex met away at school, when Alex ventured to the East Coast to study information technology and Sequoia traveled not too far from home for a school that offered a good arts education. Brown University in Rhode Island was their common ground. Coincidentally, they met during a theater production where Alex was in charge of tech and Sequoia was working on costuming and set design. It was a makeshift production of *Spunk,* and colors of the subdued south spoke to them in their earthy toned school-age love affair. They met over pizza in the school lounge. They had been together ever since, going on twenty years of togetherness with fifteen years of it as a married couple.

Grandpa Isaac muttered, "Hey, how are you?" with no real desire to know how Alex was doing. It was a nicety, and that was all it was. Alex scooted past Grandpa, losing a little swagger, and ran inside to greet his wife and little girl.

"Hey, honey, how are you?" Alex asked.

"Oh, hi, hun! How was your day?" Sequoia said.

"Okay, you won't believe this, I got a promotion!" Alex said with a sense of pride.

"My new title is IT Senior Manager."

"I'm so happy for you. I'm so happy for us. This is great!" Sequoia said.

Their kitchen led to the dining area in an open concept arrangement. Sequoia set the table for four with her favorite plates scored from Amazon Prime. She went back toward the kitchen and stirred the rice. Alex and Sequoia, blessed with struggling but stable finances, bought this two-and-some-odd-years-century-old house that they had been renovating through the years, some contract work and some do-it-yourself work, since both Alex and Sequoia were handy. Grandpa Isaac, who had the real carpenter skills, provided lots of great advice but not much actual work since his knees tended to give out on him.

"Okay, you all can sit down. Dinner is hot and ready to be eaten," Sequoia announced.

"Mom, do I have to eat the peas," Shirley said in her seventh-grade whiney voice.

Sequoia took a deep breath. "Sweetheart, you know we are having corn on the cob."

"Yes!" Shirley exclaimed.

Grandpa Isaac heard the commotion and asked, "What's all the noise about?"

"Oh, nothing, Grandpa, Mom just said we are having corn on the cob instead of peas."

"Well, that's something to celebrate," Grandpa Isaac said with cheer.

Alex snuck in with a kind of skip in his step and grabbed a biscuit and put it down on his plate. Grandpa Isaac reached for the oven-roasted chicken rolled in Sequoia's special cornflake spice mixture. Shirley heaped mounds of rice onto her plate in anticipation of the soft buttery flavor of her mom's cooked rice. Sequoia just sat down into her seat, letting a day's worth of stress melt away.

CHAPTER 3

"Dad, can you pass the corn?" Shirley blurted out.

"Sure, sweetie."

"After I hand you the grub, I've got an announcement to make." Alex extended his arm across the table as a way of breaking bread and then began to clear his throat.

"Today, I got a promotion at work. My new title is Senior IT Manager. I will take on a leadership role at the company with a pretty good pay increase."

"Congratulations, Daddy!"

"I'm so proud of you, Alex," Sequoia said.

Grandpa Isaac paused to think before he spoke. "Alex, I'm proud of you too. You have worked hard to provide for this family," Grandpa Isaac said as a peace offering of sorts.

"Thank you, everyone. I can't help but be excited. As a treat, I'm going to take us all out for ice cream after dinner."

"Thanks, Daddy, and I don't even have to eat peas."

"Enough about the peas, or we'll have them every day for dinner," Sequoia said jokingly.

"Not funny, Mom."

"Would you two old birds give it a rest?" Grandpa Isaac snapped. "We're supposed to be celebrating."

"Speaking of celebrating, I've got some news of my own," Sequoia announced.

Sequoia had been working hard all-day hustling on the phone to make things happen for her freelance work. Although she had places in town where her artwork was on display or sold in tourist shops, she hadn't had much luck getting into local museums and galleries. So this was her big chance to spread her wings and really fly.

The local art museum had space for a guest installation that her agent said would be appropriate for her paintings. Sequoia's mixed medium Afrocentric artwork had a feel-good air about it that would catch the eye of even the casual observer.

Days turned into months, and months turned into years. And before she knew it, her career consisted of craft shows and art walks. She was barely scraping by when it came to living a life full of an artist's passion for the game. During that time, Shirley, the light of her life, was born, and before she knew it, art had taken a back seat to the joys of raising a daughter. However, now, Shirley was making a mark of her own, and Sequoia didn't need to smother her every waking hour—something both Sequoia and Shirley found a refreshing change to their relationship.

Sequoia began to clear her throat. "We have two things to celebrate in one day."

"I was talking to my agent, and he wants me to be the guest exhibitor at the Cabot Museum. Isn't that great?"

"Honey, I'm so proud of you!" Alex exclaimed.

"Girl, you sure do know how to be the cherry on top of the cake," Grandpa Isaac said.

"Mommy, you rock!"

"I guess we will get two scoops of ice cream tonight," said Sequoia.

"Honey, if I'd known about all our good news, I would have taken us all out for dinner," Alex said.

"That's all right, Alex, I enjoy cooking."

"But what about the dishes?" Grandpa said.

"It comes with the territory," Sequoia replied.

They all devoured the chicken. Shirley polished off the rice, and Grandpa Isaac had two ears of corn. Next, they all helped clear the table, and Sequoia declared that this was a dishwasher kind of night. So after the dishwasher was full, they piled into Alex's sedan and drove off to Larry's, the best ice cream in town, which was open year-round for delectable treats.

A week later, Sequoia worked around the clock gathering pieces of her work that might be museum-worthy if she could get the finishing touches just right. Unfortunately, the pieces that she really loved had parted with years ago when she sold her soul to put food on the table. In reality, that was a hyperbole, but at times, it felt like a loss to sell a piece of artwork that you really loved. Sequoia's agent offered his suggestions as to which of Sequoia's pieces would show the best. Sequoia's artwork had an Afrocentric kind of vibe and used textures, colors, and a lyrical sense of design to lend weight to her artwork.

I really like this one, Sequoia thought to herself. It was a huge six by four-foot collage of sheet music with a shadow of a man playing his guitar painted in black ink on top of the collage. It was quite an exquisite piece of artwork that she was inspired by her father to create. Remembering back to when she was a little girl and her father would play the guitar as she danced around the room without a care in the world, these warm memories put a smile on her face. "*God, Dad, you really are the best that a little girl could ask for, despite your stubborn streak*," Sequoia mused aloud.

Sequoia adored her father in spite of the hard times they had been through as a family. Sequoia grew up with meager beginnings. After Vietnam, her dad had to start all over again. He had good carpentry skills, so he would do odd jobs for neighbors and family to supplement the earnings from his factory job. Eventually, after working for the man for so long, he finally decided to go into business for himself a couple years before Sequoia was born.

Sequoia's mom, Lily, worked as a secretary for a local real estate office. It was a true blessing that she landed this job, because it's what led them to their first home, a small fixer-upper cottage. Sequoia's dad, Isaac, performed miracles on their home, but it was gradual and piecemeal. Sequoia grew up with a leaky sink and a tarp on the roof. She didn't really reap the benefits of her dad and mom's hard work and sacrifices until her early teenage years. Jeffrey, her younger brother by two years, was always more focused on the tree fort in the backyard.

Sequoia always remembered the embroidered tops her mom would create for her or those hand-sewn dungarees that never fit quite right. Her mom and dad were inventive. They would think up something and then make it happen—Isaac with his wood skills and Lily with her sewing. It was no wonder that Sequoia got the creative bug and took to art. Jeffrey was always a numbers guy, and now he did their taxes. He moved up quickly after getting his first job out of college. It didn't hurt that he went to night school to become a CPA. As a certified public accountant, the doors opened up for him, but ultimately that independent streak rubbed off from his dad and mom. He ended up owning his own business. And what a business it was. Jeffrey wasn't one to toot his own horn, but he was living large.

CHAPTER 4

In Shirley's room, Shirley and Olivia danced around to the dynamic, joyous rhythm of the Bruno Mars hit *Uptown Funk* blasting from the speakers. Both had been dancing since before they could talk, and it was what cemented their friendship.

"I can't believe it's only three months till the talent show," Olivia said.

"Yeah, and tryouts are tomorrow," Shirley pointed out.

"I think we've got this," Olivia said.

They played the tune from start to finish as they broke down their hip-hop-funkified moves. It was clear that Shirley had a creative edge over Olivia, but Olivia's confidence carried them through. When the music stopped, Grandpa Isaac poked his head through the door and asked for a preview. The girls played the tune again and gave it their best effort. Grandpa Isaac erupted in applause as the last beats ended, and the girls broke out in laughter and smiles.

The next day after school, Olivia and Shirley changed in the girl's locker room and put on their coordinating outfits, which had a cool but comfortable vibe. When the music began to play, the light on Shirley's face lit up the auditorium, and Olivia's cool swagger added spice. At the end of their routine, the judges clapped and told them that they would post a list tomorrow of who made it through. The girls thanked the judges before running off stage.

"Well, we did it!" Olivia exclaimed.

"And it was fun, too," Shirley retorted.

Shirley could hardly sleep all night. She was filled with excitement and anticipation. Olivia was feeling the same but was a bit more self-assured. Later that night around ten, a mutual friend of Olivia and Shirley texted Olivia a picture of Shirley with AJ that said, "*Shirley and AJ make love child alien baby!*" Olivia chuckled, thinking it was cute, in a playful kind of way, and decided to post it to Instagram and Snapchat. Well, little did she know that the picture went practically viral overnight. The entire seventh grade was talking about it from early morning to late afternoon. It wasn't until the second period that Shirley got wind of it.

"What's so funny, Missy?" Shirley nagged.

"You mean you didn't see the picture?" Missy said with surprise. "I thought you knew."

"Knew what?" Shirley said.

"I'm sorry, Shirley, I shouldn't have laughed," Missy gulped.

"Just show me!" Shirley said impatiently.

Missy, being the good friend that she was, didn't want to leave Shirley in the dark, but then at the same time, she didn't want to break the bad news to her either.

"Okay, Shirley, I'll show you the picture, but I had nothing to do with it. You need to talk to Olivia," Missy said with reluctance.

Then Missy showed her the picture of her and AJ with the caption, "*Shirley and AJ make love child alien baby!*" In shock and terribly saddened, Shirley tried to stop the tears that she could feel coming. As the kind of kid who would do anything for anybody, Shirley might be described as *too nice*.

Tears welled up in Shirley's eyes, and she immediately excused herself to the bathroom. Missy followed her and tried to comfort her, by letting her know that she was sorry she even looked at the picture.

Suddenly, Shirley's sadness turned to fury, "Who started this rumor?"

Missy hesitated to answer and then said, "Jackie made the picture, and Olivia spread it on Instagram and Snapchat."

Shirley couldn't believe it, one of her closest friends tried to ruin her life. *But why?* she thought. Then she remembered about the talent show and remembered that she forgot to check the posting that showed the list. Through her tears, she told Missy about the talent show tryouts and how the list should be posted, just as the bell of the end of second period rang. Shirley dried her eyes, grabbed her books from second period with Missy, and ran to the talent show list. Missy read the list to her and said, "You made it!"

Shirley was filled with dismay and feelings of mixed emotions, and just then, Olivia bumped into her and said, "Hey, stranger."

Shirley barked, "What's that supposed to mean?"

"It means, I haven't seen you all morning, what gives?"

"What gives!" Shirley wasn't one to call names, but she couldn't control what her hormones were about to do.

"You witch!" Shirley yelled at the top of her lungs, as she wound up and slapped Olivia across the face.

Olivia immediately cowered and got Mrs. Wilder and told her what had happened. Mrs. Wilder, knowing both girls' characters, wondered what had provoked Shirley to do such a thing. Shirley explained what Olivia had done. Ms. Wilder said she wanted to see both girls after school, and she was going to email both of their parents right away. Shirley dreaded the end of the day and barely made it through the rest of her classes. She reported to Mrs. Wilder's room at the end of the day to find Olivia sitting at the other end of the room.

Mrs. Wilder pulled both girls aside separately and spoke to them. Shirley's eyes watered with embarrassment, sadness, and a little rage. However, Olivia was eerily calm and calculated. She was the more manipulative of the two. For the rest of the hour after school, Shirley and Olivia worked on homework on opposite ends of the room. At three o'clock, Mrs. Wilder released both of them and said, "Remember, it pays to be kind." This resonated with Shirley but didn't faze Olivia at all.

The two girls parted ways, hoping never to speak to one another again. All those memories over their eight-year friendship had been washed away. Olivia yearned for the kindness Shirley always showered on her. Shirley was Olivia's only true friend who knew her deepest secrets in and out. Shirley missed Olivia's joking and the laughter that always accompanied her. But this friendship was over. It was all in the past. If there was anything that preadolescent girls were good at, it was holding grudges.

A strong hand stroked Shirley on the shoulder, and a soft gruff reassuring voice said, "Hey, sweets."

"Grandpa!" Shirley exclaimed with genuine excitement for the first time all day.

"I thought mom was going to pick me up." Shirley remembered Mrs. Wilder's email.

"Your mom got caught up with an errand she had to run, so you got me instead."

"How's you say we take the long way home today," Grandpa Isaac said with concern and empathy in his eyes.

"Okay."

Shirley and Grandpa Isaac were pretty much silent on the way home, but it was an understanding silence. When they got to their street, Shirley burst out in tears and explained everything that had happened throughout a day that had felt like a year. Grandpa Isaac listened and stroked Shirley's arm with loving care. It was all he could do to not to cry for her as he could feel the hurt she was feeling.

"Sugar, all I know is that there's nothing worse than getting burned by a friend, especially when that friend was a trusted companion," Grandpa Isaac said. Though he only half-believed what he said as he never really trusted Olivia completely. He always knew that Shirley was all too kind in the midst of Olivia's cool, self-assured presence.

Then Shirley confessed, "I loved her like a sister."

Shirley said this as she reminisced in her mind about the good times spent with her former friend, Olivia.

Then Shirley remembered three years ago when Shirley and Olivia made a birthday cake for her mom. They followed the recipe to a tee, but Olivia wanted to add some flare. So she said, "Let's add a couple of tablespoons of ginger and cinnamon, and we can call it Shirley and Olivia's Special Surprise." Well, when mom bit into that cake, boy was it a special surprise. Shirley couldn't help but smile at the thought of this memory.

Grandpa Isaac was quiet as Shirley stared off out her window while deep in thought. Shirley kept filing through her Olivia memories before feeling a shiver of betrayal as she remembered the stares and looks she got all day as kids at school got wind of the viral rumor. Eventually, Grandpa Isaac and Shirley got out of the car and moseyed into the house and snuck away to their corners. Grandpa Isaac tried to get Shirley to spend some time out of her room, but Shirley was insistent about spending time by herself in her room, watching old reruns on Netflix.

Later, Shirley's mom came home, about an hour before her dad arrived, and her mom had a heart-to-heart with Shirley. Shirley told her mom what happened but did not express the feelings and emotions that were rushing through her body ranging from embarrassment to shame to anger, and then of course, there was a deep sadness for the loss of her friend—the loss of a well-worn friendship soon to be thrown to the wayside.

Shirley soon became emerged in this sadness and couldn't find her way out of it. Two weeks had gone by, and Shirley had made a trend of school, home, and room. School was a nightmare, because she was still teased about the alien baby meme. Missy was her only friend she could count on at school. Home was dysfunctional and distancing because mom was busy with her art exhibit and dad was consumed with work. Grandpa Isaac was a comforting companion, but something had changed about him too. Shirley noticed he went to one too many doctor's appointments lately. Shirley's room had truly become her sanctuary, where she would vibe out to music or zone out watching her favorite shows. Life had become a nightmare, and Shirley could not wake up.

CHAPTER 5

It was Saturday morning in the Johnson household, and everyone was busy, everyone of course but Shirley. Sequoia, Shirley's mom, was working on her museum exhibit installation. Shirley's dad was playing a few rounds of golf with some work buddies, and Grandpa Isaac had to run to the doctor for some blood work. Shirley's mom came into her room, kissed her on the forehead, and reassured her that she would be back later in the day. She promised that Shirley could help her cook dinner tonight, one of her favorites, homemade mac 'n' cheese.

Having the house to herself used to be fun because Shirley would invite her friend Olivia over, and they would blast their dance music and dance around the living room. Without Olivia, having the house to herself was no longer fun. It was just lonely. Shirley couldn't even think of dancing anymore. She would listen to her music intently without feeling an ounce of happiness. In fact, Shirley spent much of her day crying, listening to sad music, and watching depressing movies on TV. When her mom came home around four in the afternoon, she found Shirley, lying in bed with tears in her eyes staring at her phone.

"Shirley, what is going on?" her mom said.

"Nothing, Mom," Shirley moaned.

"I'm going to have a word with your father about this," Shirley's Mom said as she left the room.

Shirley pulled the covers up over her head and sobbed. It was a deep sob, one that filled her heart with sadness, for it was the loss that really made her yearn. Shirley's mom forgot completely about making the mac 'n' cheese and settled on takeout for supper. When Alex came home, Sequoia told him, "Honey, we need to talk." And talk they did, for about an hour. Alex and Sequoia discussed Shirley's new apathetic behaviors.

"Honey," Alex said, "I really think she's depressed."

"I do, too, but what do we do about it?" Sequoia said with concern.

Then Alex and Sequoia started discussing their options. They talked about having a conversation with the social worker at school. They talked about getting her involved in sports, but then they settled on family counseling. They both agreed that their family could use some much-needed instruction on how to communicate better, and they needed to get Shirley talking about her feelings instead of spending the day in bed sobbing. Sequoia was right on it, so she scheduled an appointment for the upcoming Wednesday afternoon. Sequoia mentioned to Alex it might be nice if she invited Grandpa Isaac to come along, since he was so close to Shirley. Alex agreed.

Wednesday arrived, and when Shirley got home from school, they all piled into Alex's sedan and made their way across town to the appointment. Grandpa Isaac was stoic and didn't mumble a word, as he had reservations about this sort of therapy. He wanted to get Shirley some needed help, but he didn't know if it would be necessary to put them all under a microscope. As they arrived at the therapist's office, Sequoia took the lead on filling out the necessary paperwork.

Shirley seemed like she was in a trance as she did not have a clue as to what they were getting into as her mom said that she thought that they should all go as a family to talk to someone about learning how to communicate better. When they called the family to come into the office to meet the therapist, Shirley's heart sank. She kept thinking to herself, *What would they talk about? Would they blame her for the family's problems? Should she even speak at all?*

Soon enough, all Shirley's questions were answered in an hour-and-a-half session, where they just talked. Talked about how they were feeling, talked about their joys and their concerns, talked about their hopes and fears, and Grandpa Isaac even told some funny jokes. It felt like they were at the dinner table, but instead of the fluffy arguments, they got to the meat of the conversation and just opened up and talked. It was almost like the office was a safe space, and whatever happened in the office was safe to talk about, because Dr. Jones acted as a referee of sorts, a mediator, someone who didn't have any skin in the game.

Shirley was almost sad when the session was over and looked forward to next week when they would meet again. Dr. Jones gave them a slip and said, "See you next Wednesday at the end of the session." Then, after the session, Alex sprang for Mickey D's, and Shirley had a double cheeseburger, fries, and a small shake—a day's worth of calories all in one meal. Little did Shirley know that she would soon be working those calories off with a surprise dance session.

As soon as they got home, Grandpa Isaac asked Shirley to come into the family room with him. The family room was a big sunny room with wooden floors, a throw rug, and comfy couches. Grandpa Isaac had the couches pushed back against the outer walls of the room, and he had the throw rug rolled up and a kitchen chair in the corner of the room with his guitar leaning up against it.

"Grandpa, what are you up to?" Shirley inquired.

"Nothing much, I just thought you'd like to put those pretty little dancing shoes on again."

"Where's the music?" Shirley pleaded.

"I thought I'd play for you," Grandpa Isaac grinned.

Grandpa Isaac picked up the guitar and started to play soft pleasantries that were soothing to even the weariest of hearts. Shirley was timid at first, and then she took off her socks and shoes and stood barefooted among the playing of Grandpa Isaac's music and decided to dance along. She stretched out her legs and raised her arms and curved her back and made sharp and soft movements all at the same time. Shirley was a skilled dancer, semiprofessional if you will. She knew how to lyricize her body to the music in a way that conveyed her feelings. Although before today, Grandpa Isaac had rarely played his guitar for her as he said it brought back too many memories, good and sad. Shirley guessed that he was talking about Grandma Lily, but you could never be too sure with Grandpa, as his mind was like a vault of memories.

At one point, Grandpa Isaac even sang along to some of Shirley's favorite cover songs as he strummed the chords in a melodic kind of way. After some time, Grandpa Isaac sensed Shirley's fatigue and slowed the music down before he stopped playing. Shirley stopped dancing, ran over to Grandpa Isaac, gave him a big hug, and whispered, "*Thank you.*" Shirley and Grandpa Isaac had an understanding of sorts, a connection that united them in spirit. Grandpa Isaac began to clean up the family room, and Shirley helped him in a laughing playful game they created. Shirley was in a really good mood and felt refreshed by finally being able to dance again.

Grandpa Isaac said to Shirley, "What about that talent show of yours?"

Shirley took a moment and then replied, "I just gave up on it since Olivia and I aren't friends anymore."

"Well, why don't you enter on your own?" Grandpa Isaac asked.

"I never thought of that before. I'm a little nervous about going solo," Shirley replied.

"Sometimes we have to face our fears in order to make progress, why don't you give it a shot!"

"Will you do it with me? I mean, will you play the guitar for me?" Shirley asked anxiously.

Grandpa Isaac smiled with pride as he answered, "I would love too."

"Great!" Shirley said as she hugged Grandpa Isaac tightly.

The next day, Shirley went into school excited for the first time in a while. She marched down to the Performing Arts office and let them know that she was still going to enter the talent show but on her own. She also let them know that her grandfather would be playing the guitar for her instead of canned music. The woman in charge said that was fine and wrote down Shirley's information. She let her know that there would be a couple of rehearsal days coming up and also let Shirley know that there were to be no risqué costumes—all outfits needed to meet school dress code. Shirley thanked the teacher and continued with her day. When Shirley got home from school excited to let Grandpa Isaac know her good news, Grandpa Isaac wasn't home. Her mom was in the kitchen.

"Hi, Mom," Shirley said with surprise in her voice.

"Hi, honey, how was school today?"

"It was great!" Shirley said excitedly.

"Oh, honey, I'm so glad school is going well."

Then Shirley couldn't contain herself anymore and blurted her good news out, "I entered the talent show on my own, and Grandpa Isaac is going to play the guitar for me. I'm so excited!"

"Oh my gosh, honey, this is such great news!" Sequoia said.

"You know you are quite the artist," Sequoia said to Shirley.

"Artist? Mom, don't you mean dancer?"

"No, Shirley, I mean artist."

Then, Shirley and her mom had a long discussion about what it means to be an artist. Sequoia expressed the importance of having a creative outlet and that we all have unique voices and presence in art. She also said that art takes different shapes and molds, and it is not limited to visual arts. Then Shirley asked how dance fit into the art world. Her mom explained that dance was a type of performing arts, which allowed people to express themselves through movement. Shirley was amazed, because all this time while she had loved dance and excelled at it, she never once considered herself an artist. She just thought of dance as something that she did, something that she loved to do. This discussion with her mom changed her whole perspective on her art, dance.

CHAPTER 6

A week later, Shirley came home from school and her mom was there getting things ready for her exhibition that was opening the coming weekend. Friday night was the meet and greet at the art museum, and Shirley was so excited to go, since it was a dressy, grown-up affair.

"How goes it, Mom?" Shirley asked as she grabbed the reddest apple from the fruit bowl.

"Oh hi, honey, how was school?"

"It was great. I'm learning about negative numbers," Shirley shared.

"Better you than me," said Sequoia. "I'm not as good at math as you are."

"Where's Grandpa?" Shirley asked

"He's in the other room lying down," Sequoia said casually.

"Oh, I guess I'll talk to him later."

"Oh Mom, do you think I can get a new dress for tomorrow?"

"Sure, Shirley, that's a good idea. I need to pick up some shoes as well. The heel broke on my favorite pair of pumps."

Shirley and her mom left for the mall and shopped for an hour or two. Shirley found a flowy light floral dress, and her mom found a pair of metallic pumps resembling the inside pattern of an oyster shell, a perfect match for her A-line powder blue dress.

When Shirley got home, she ran into Grandpa Isaac's room and showed him her new dress. Grandpa Isaac let out a big yawn and then excitedly let Shirley know that she would be quite the princess in her new dress.

"You clean up like Cinderella," said Grandpa Isaac jokingly.

"Not funny," said Shirley.

"I can't wait till tomorrow!" exclaimed Shirley.

"Yeah, I'm looking forward to it myself," Grandpa Isaac said as he gave Shirley a squeeze.

It was Friday night, and Sequoia headed out early to finish up some last-minute things before the big exhibition. Decked to the nines and looking sharp, Alex, Shirley, and Grandpa Isaac piled into Alex's sedan. Grandpa Isaac cleaned up well. Shirley looked just like the princess Grandpa Isaac said she was, and Alex looked like he could be on the cover of GQ magazine.

They arrived at the museum a few minutes before the event started and waited patiently for the meet-and-greet exhibition to begin. At seven o'clock, the exhibition opened with hor d'oeuvres being served while patrons perused the exhibition and chatted with Sequoia. The museum was lit up with vibrant colors, patterns, and textures. Sequoia's style was Afrocentric with a bit of Caribbean flavor. When Sequoia spied her dad, Alex, and Shirley, she excused herself and ran over full of excitement.

"I'm so glad to see you all!" Sequoia exclaimed.

"Wow, you *are* good!" Grandpa Isaac proclaimed.

"You sure are!" Alex agreed.

"I agree, Mommy, you are a spectacular artist!" Shirley exclaimed as she hugged her mother.

"Well, I hope you all enjoy yourselves," Sequoia said with kindness. "I have to mingle. I'll see you all at home."

A Caribbean jazz ensemble played live music while guests experienced the exhibit, enjoying art, good food, and ambiance, not to mention good conversations with like-minded art enthusiasts. Shirley, Alex, and Grandpa Isaac really enjoyed themselves and marveled at their dear Sequoia's artwork. Shirley ranked her favorite artwork from favorite to absolutely most awesome of all. Then Shirley conversed with her dad and Grandpa Isaac about how she's an artist too as she explained how dance is an art form.

"Wow, I'm impressed Shirley," said Grandpa Isaac.

"You seem to know an awful lot about art," said Alex. Shirley's dad admired his daughter's wide-ranging knowledge of art.

"Mom and I had a long chat about what it means to be an artist, and how creativity flows in different forms," Shirley said, very adult-like.

A half-hour later, around nine o'clock, Shirley, Grandpa Isaac, and Alex headed out. They waved goodbye to Sequoia, and she headed over and kissed them goodbye and thanked them for coming. Grandpa Isaac reassured his daughter that the pleasure was all theirs and that her talent was one to be reckoned with. Sequoia blushed at his flattery and then disappeared into the crowd. It was an exceptionally good turn out, and the museum was hopping with patrons.

The exhibition didn't wrap up until around ten o'clock, but Sequoia didn't head home until about eleven. When she got home, the house was buzzing with enthusiasm and excitement. The family was extremely proud of Sequoia as they watched her dreams come true. All those years of being a struggling artist were finally paying off as she was beginning to make a name for herself. However, Sequoia remained humble and kind and gave credit to her talent as coming from a higher power.

CHAPTER 7

A few weeks later, Shirley and Grandpa Isaac began to prepare for the talent show. Shirley and Grandpa Isaac had been rehearsing at home and at school. Just the previous week, they had completed two rehearsals at the school. Now, on Wednesday evening, they were working out the kinks in the family room so that things would run smoothly at the show Thursday afternoon. It was hard to believe that after weeks of rehearsal, the show was just a day away.

"Grandpa, do you think things will go well tomorrow?" Shirley questioned.

"We'll be dy-no-mite!" he said.

They continued to run the rehearsal. Grandpa Isaac played his guitar, while Shirley danced and danced. The music was jazzy lyrical, just like Shirley's dance. She had chosen a flowy all-white dress to wear with dance pants under it for comfort and coverage. The run-through went off without a hitch, and Shirley and Grandpa Isaac were in sync.

That night at supper, Shirley's mom had a million questions about how the dance was going. Grandpa Isaac told Sequoia that she'd just have to wait and see. Alex was curious but knew better than to pester them. However, Alex was pretty stoked about going to the show.

The night passed, and Thursday morning at school, Shirley felt like a nervous wreck filled with good excitement. Missy stuck by Shirley's side most of the morning, anxiously awaiting the talent show scheduled after lunch at one o'clock. Shirley's mom and dad took the afternoon off to attend the show. The annual talent show was a big event that drew people from the entire community. The show offered students dancing, singing, performing magic, playing instruments, and much more.

The school celebrated the variety of talent but also didn't mind dabbling in a little healthy competition. Consequently, the first-place winner would receive a $250 cash prize. The second-place winner received $100, and the third-place winner received $50. There were fifteen acts in the talent show, all vetted ahead of time, as they had to try out for the show. This meant that the contestants were the cream of the crop. The students were highly skilled, and even people with no artistic talent recognized how impressive they were.

It was twelve thirty, and students were beginning to be dismissed to the auditorium. Parents, families, and community members were beginning to arrive. The auditorium was packed. As a school that specialized in and valued the performing arts, it had an extremely large auditorium. Shirley and Grandpa Isaac were in the backstage area with the other acts. Shirley met eyes with Olivia who was one of the other dance acts with a group of three girls. They were doing a hip-hop dance similar to what Shirley and Olivia were going to do to *Uptown Funk* (she basically stole Shirley's moves).

Grandpa Isaac rubbed Shirley's shoulders and said, "You're going to do great, kiddo, knock 'em dead."

This set Shirley at ease, and she took three deep breaths and said, "I hope you're right."

It was nearing one o'clock, and the show was just beginning. The MC hammed up the show, and the acts were on their way. Shirley and Grandpa Isaac closed the show. As the very last act to go on stage, waiting had set Shirley's nerves on fire, but after the performance, the show was over.

The first act was a girl with a showstopping voice, which got a roar of applause after her performance. Then there was a drum player who brought a little rock 'n' roll to the show. After that, there were magic acts, more singers, dancers, and entertaining performers. It was a little after two, and the act before Shirley and Grandpa Isaac was on. He was a violinist who was quite good. The last chords of his song rang in Shirley's head as she had the music memorized as it was her cue for when she was to go on. The violinist finished, and the crowd roared. Shirley held Grandpa Isaac's hand and gave it a little squeeze as the MC announced the act, and Shirley and Grandpa Isaac walked out on stage. Shirley's mom and dad must have gotten there early because they were in the second row.

There was a chair on the stage set to the side, which is where Grandpa Isaac sat with a microphone adjusted to the level of the guitar. The rest of the stage was Shirley's. Grandpa Isaac began to play, and Shirley began to move with the white dress flowing, coordinated with the fuchsia flower in her hair. The sound was melodic and smooth, just like Shirley's movements. She moved with grace and maturity. She danced beyond her years. The dance moves came easy to her as did her flexibility.

As the music crescendoed, so did her movements. She began to spin faster and faster and then erupted into a split leap that had everyone erupting in applause as she finished the last movements of the dance. When Shirley took her bow with Grandpa Isaac, she rose to a standing ovation that made it clear that their dance act was a hit.

Tears fell from both Sequoia and Alex's eyes as they stood and applauded their baby girl. Although, one would have to say they were not the only ones crying in the house. Grandpa Isaac's music and Shirley's movements touched people in a way that could not be explained. It may be why so many people responded so emotionally to their performance. After a minute or two, Shirley and Grandpa Isaac rushed to the wings offstage and waited for their cue, as all the acts were supposed to join back on stage. The announcer had a stand-up act and some games and riddles for the audience while the judges made their final decisions about who the top three acts were and who won the talent show.

Ten minutes later, Grandpa Isaac and Shirley as well as the other acts were called back on stage for the announcement of the winners. The fifteen acts were spread across the stage and lit up the place with color and flare. As some of the best of the best, no one would really go home a loser. The third-place winner was the rock 'n' roll drummer who brought down the house. Then the runner-up was the violinist who had strokes of genius. Then last but not least, the winner of the talent show was Shirley and Grandpa

Isaac. When they announced her name, Shirley was shocked. As she moved forward, tears of joy slowly rolled down her cheeks as she accepted her flowers, the check for $250, as well as a trophy, which Shirley handed to Grandpa Isaac to hold. Shirley just kept uttering, "Thank you," over and over again.

Minutes later, they were backstage, and lo and behold who did Shirley bump into, but Olivia. Olivia began to stutter out a congratulations and an apology for what had happened between them. Shirley was taken aback, as she was still heartbroken over the loss of their friendship and hurt from the betrayal of such a close friend. However, the words *thanks* slowly slumbered out of Shirley's mouth. Then Shirley let Olivia know that she needed to go and find her mom and dad. Olivia said she understood as they parted ways. Grandpa Isaac stood at an earshot's distance and listened with interest. He let Shirley know that he was proud of her for being kind. "Remember that forgiveness is knowing that the very worst part of you is good again, because you let your heart heal, by giving someone else grace." Then Shirley gave Grandpa Isaac a squeeze and a kiss on the cheek, as Shirley said, "Let's go find Mom and Dad."

Shirley and Grandpa Isaac set foot into the crowd of people in the auditorium showering them with accolades. Shirley stayed focused on finding her mom and dad. Then she saw them with pink puffy eyes. They shouted to her, "Shirley!" Then they all embraced, and even Grandpa Isaac joined in.

"We are so proud of you both!" Sequoia erupted with excitement.

"I was brought to tears," Alex said with candor.

Then Grandpa Isaac chimed in, "Shirley brought down the house!"

"Well, I had a little help," said Shirley, as they all erupted into laughter.

"Let's get out of here," Alex said. There was a crowd of people at the door, so Alex led the way with a mouthful of *excuse me* and a gentle push. Before going out to the car, Alex suggested that they get all dolled up when they get home, because he was treating them all to a fancy dinner at one of the five-star Afro-Caribbean restaurants in town. Shirley jumped for joy. Grandpa Isaac smiled and said, "You're not so bad of a guy, you know that, Alex." Alex smiled and gave Grandpa Isaac a thumbs up. Then they parted ways, headed toward their cars, and went home to get ready for their special dinner.

CHAPTER 8

They arrived at the restaurant and waited for twenty minutes as Alex got them a last-minute reservation for their impromptu celebration dinner. After they were seated, Shirley whispered to Grandpa, "What do I do with my napkin?"

Grandpa Isaac slyly replied, "You use it." Shirley rolled her eyes at Grandpa Isaac, so he then responded by modeling for her by neatly placing the napkin in his lap. Shirley replied, "Thanks," and stared in awe at the chandelier lighting fixtures that twinkled with crystal. Alex noticed Shirley's entranced look. He smiled and then nudged Sequoia. She started a conversation with Shirley about how sometimes it's fun to splurge.

Then she asked Shirley, "What are you going to do with your $250 winnings?"

Shirley hesitated to answer and then said, "I've been thinking a lot about it, and I am very lucky to have taken dance classes all my life. Some people might like dance and don't realize it because they can't afford the tuition. I think I want to start an after-school arts program for little kids with dance, art, music, and theater that would cost nothing to go to. I don't know the details, but I'd like to donate the money."

"I think what you're talking about is a nonprofit," said Sequoia.

"I can see if work would sponsor you or donate some money," piped in Alex.

"And I can donate my time, so long as I am well enough," said Grandpa Isaac as the words slipped out of his mouth.

"What do you mean, *well enough*?" questioned Sequoia.

"I didn't mean to bring that up now," said Grandpa Isaac.

Just in the nick of time, the waiter delivered their food with a flare. They all erupted with smiles, laughter, and thank-yous as they identified which meal belonged to each of them. They all began to eat, savoring every bite. The food had a spicy taste married with a divine flavor and was just what they needed. However, Sequoia's keen sense of intuition wouldn't allow her to ignore her dad's words, *well enough*. "Dad," she said, "tell me the truth, are you sick?" Sequoia, lost in concern, forgot about her thirteen-year-old's presence for a moment.

"I have prostate cancer," Grandpa Isaac said candidly, "but I have a good treatment plan, and I will start chemo and radiation soon."

"God, Dad, why don't you ever tell me anything?"

"Because I didn't want to worry you."

Alex clamored in to save the day, "Let's remember this is a celebration dinner. We can discuss this at another time."

Shirley was silent during this whole conversation. She just listened intently, as she had nothing but love for her grandfather. As they ate their dinner, they talked about Shirley's dancing skills, Grandpa Isaac's amazing guitar playing, Sequoia's skill in the visual arts, and Alex's behind-the-scenes production and strategy. Sequoia was pretty keen on her daughter's idea about an after-school program that turned into a nonprofit. They brainstormed and dreamed up real-life solutions to turn this $250 dream into reality.

Weeks went by, and Sequoia, Shirley, Alex, and Grandpa Isaac worked on the after-school arts program and turned it into a reality. School was almost out for the year, so they decided to offer a summer arts program. Alex got his company as well as some other local businesses to sponsor the program. Sequoia got local artists to teach and donate their time into a time bank, which they could cash in on other talents. For example, if you teach dance for five hours, you can cash it in for an hour class in pottery or piano lessons. The classes are free for the local kids. It was a really great program.

On the other front, Grandpa Isaac started chemo and radiation. His prognosis was good, despite his exhaustion and fatigue. He promised to contribute music classes as soon as he was well enough to play. But in the meantime, he would watch Shirley and Sequoia do their thing teaching dance and art. It was really great seeing the creative juices of his young ones flow.

Shirley came into Grandpa Isaac's room and lay down next to him. He opened his eyes and uttered the words, "Hey, beautiful." Shirley gave his hand a squeeze and smiled.

"I love you, Grandpa Isaac."

"Ditto, sweetheart. I mean, I love you too."

"Don't ever let go of my hand, Grandpa."

"Don't ever let go of my heart," Grandpa Isaac said with clarity.

"I won't," Shirley reassured Grandpa Isaac as she gave his hand another squeeze.

ABOUT THE AUTHOR

Alice-Marie is a new African American female author with stories to tell. A little bit about her—she is a mom of two adventurous young adult boys. Career-wise, she is a special education teacher for twelve years and has been working in the education field for eighteen years. She recently just received her doctorate in educational leadership. She has a passion for writing and an interest in nonconventional creative writing. Her inspirations are Ntozake Shange and Zora Neale Hurston (not to mention she loves a little Toni Morrison). Words are like clay to her. She says you can shape them and mold them into a pottery extravaganza.